Elean

The
Vicarage
Rats

Scripture Union

By the same author:
Sam's kind of dog – Tiger
Keep Out! – Tiger
The Next Door Zoo – Tiger
Nobody's dog – Read by Myself

First published 1997

Scripture Union, 207–209 Queensway, Bletchley,
Milton Keynes, MK2 2EB, England.

ISBN 1 85999 069 X

British Library Cataloguing-in-Publication Data.
A catalogue record of this book is available from the
British Library.

Printed and bound in Great Britain by Cox & Wyman
Ltd, Reading.

Contents

Chapter one
Moving day

Tom was writing to Grandma, squeezed up on the window seat with an exercise book on his knees.

"Dear Gran, We arived about 3 o clock. The van got lost so we haven't any beds. The house is all emty. If you shout it eckos. Emma was sick in the car. Its cold here. I think ..."

The next words to write were already in his head, waiting to tumble out on to the paper. *"I think our old house was much nicer. It was nice and warm. I miss it. I miss Brian and Kevin. I miss you, Gran ..."*

But before he could write them, he was interrupted by a shriek from Emma. She had been swinging on the stripped-pine door of the new living-room, listening to the interesting squeak it made, and had managed to pinch her fingers. Mum and Dad rushed in from the kitchen, where they had been sorting out water and a kettle to make a cup of tea, which was the only thing they could do until the furniture caught up with them.

"Emma," said Mum, gathering up her sobbing child. "Never mind. It's only a little pinch. Nothing to cry about."

Tom thought that Mum looked as though she

5

might cry herself, clutching Emma and looking round the bare room. The removal van had taken a wrong turn, gone miles out of its way and was now parked in a lay-by for the night, as it was getting dark already. They'd have to manage without furniture for tonight.

Also, it seemed that the electricity hadn't been connected. Dad came in from the kitchen and said so. He picked up the phone from the floor, muttering that at least something was working, and made a cross-sounding call to the electricity people.

"Tomorrow, at the earliest," he said gloomily. Then his face brightened, because the rest of them were looking gloomy, and someone ought to stay cheerful.

"It's not the end of the world. Tom, come and help me chop up that old packing case, the one we brought the kettle and saucepans in. It's almost falling to bits anyway. We'll make a fire in the fireplace. It'll be fun, like camping."

The big empty room did look better when flames were leaping up into the chimney and crackling merrily. Mum found candles and stuck them into some old jamjars she had discovered in the shed. The flames wavered in the draught from the fire and sent shadows flickering into the corners of the room. Emma clutched her favourite rag doll and sat on the carpet with her thumb in her mouth, watching the flames. Her blonde hair looked red-gold in the firelight.

The door slammed and there were footsteps in the hall. Peter came in on a rush of cold air, with Rusty on the lead. Peter was ten now, old enough to walk the dog by himself, even in a strange, new town. Rusty came and leaned against Tom, his coat smelling of cold and the outdoors. Tom hugged him. Rusty was partly Red Setter but not altogether. He was always a comfort if you were a bit lonely or sad.

"This is great!" said Peter, holding out his hands to the fire. "It's cold out there. I'm hungry, though. What's for tea?"

Mum and Dad had boiled a pan of water and made tea, with biscuits from the packet of supplies they'd brought in the car.

But after a long day's travelling, everyone was in need of something more substantial.

"There's a takeaway in the next street but one, just on the corner," said Peter. 'I'll go, if you like."

Mum said that it was too dark now for him to go alone, so he and Dad went together. Everyone felt much better when they had a hot meal inside them. Emma fell asleep, and Mum got one of the sleeping-bags from the car and bundled her into it.

"It's sleeping-bags on the floor all round tonight," said Dad, bringing in an armful of pillows and cushions. "In fact, we could all sleep right here, together, in the living-room. It'll at least be a bit warmer."

The fire was dying down and there was no more wood to keep it going. The room was beginning to feel chilly again.

"I'd like to sleep upstairs, in my new room," said Peter. "Coming, Tom?"

Tom would have preferred to be with the rest of the family, on the first night in that strange, chilly, echoing new home, or at least have Rusty with them. But Mum was very strict about dogs

7

sleeping in bedrooms. He said, "Yes, I'm coming," and followed his brother up the creaking, shadowy stairs with only the light from Peter's torch to see the way, leaving Mum, Dad, and Emma to share the living-room, and Rusty in the kitchen.

They undressed by torch light and crept shivering into the sleeping-bags, wriggling about to get the most comfortable position on the carpet.

"It's nice here," said Peter. "Shove over, Tom, don't squash up to me like that. You scared or something?"

"Course not," said Tom. "Just a bit cold." He moved away a little, but shifted up again in the sleeping-bag when he thought Peter had gone to sleep. It was odd, having the window behind them and not in front as it had been in their old room in the old house.

Thinking about the old house made a big lump come up in Tom's throat. Peter might like it here, but he wasn't sure he did. Not sure at all. Their furniture and beds and bikes and belongings might be here tomorrow, but his friends Kevin and Brian were hundreds of miles away. And so was Gran.

Gran had lived just around the corner from the old house. Her house wasn't really a country cottage but it looked like one, set back from the road in a garden full of roses and geraniums. Gran lived with Pickle, her cat, who had a bit missing from the end of his tail after a fight. Gran played games with them, long drawn-out games like *Scrabble* and *Monopoly*, that no one else ever had time to play. She always won at *Scrabble*, but Peter was just beginning to beat her at *Monopoly* sometimes. Gran had a vegetable patch in her back garden, but let the grass grow over most of it so that the boys could have a cricket pitch. She was quite good at batting when they played cricket, an excellent fielder, but not quite such a fast runner as she used to be. But when Peter had hit the ball into the next-door garden, it was Gran who'd climbed over and nipped back with it before anyone noticed and complained.

Thinking of Gran almost made him cry properly. He did sniffle a bit, but pretended that the cold air was making his nose run, and wiped it on his pyjama sleeve. However would they manage with Gran so far away?

It was Gran who'd quite often taken him to church with her back home, and who'd taught him to say his prayers. She always said "Remember, Tom, talking to God is just like talking to your best friend. You don't ever have to pretend with God, because he loves you whether you're good or bad, or happy or sad, or whatever. Just tell him exactly how you feel. And ask him anything you like. He's always listening out for you."

He said, under his breath, "God, I don't like this new house, much. I miss Gran and I miss my friends. I want to go home."

And then he sniffled a bit more and had to wipe his nose again.

Chapter two
A midnight message

Tom didn't remember falling asleep, but he must have because he woke with a jump all of a sudden. Something had made a noise at the window.

Tom put out his hand quickly to where Peter should have been, but there was just a limp, empty sleeping-bag with no Peter in it. Then he saw the outline of his brother standing at the window, looking down into the dark front garden to see what had made the noise. A cold draught showed that he had opened the window.

"Peter!" said Tom.

Peter turned, talking in a half-whisper. "Ssh! There's someone there. They threw some gravel at the window.

Tom's heart began to thump. "Is it burglars?" he asked.

"'Course not, silly! They wouldn't wake us up on purpose. Besides, there's nothing here to burgle. I think it's some boys—"

At that moment, something else came hurtling past Peter through the open window, landing with a thud on the carpet. Tom couldn't hold back a frightened squeak.

"Ssh!" said Peter again. "It's only a ball, I think.

They've gone now. Let's have a look."

He closed the window and fumbled for his torch. Its thin yellow beam showed a bright green tennis ball, and, wrapped around it, a piece of paper secured by a rubber band.

"It's a message!" whispered Peter.

Tom sat up in the sleeping-bag, half scared and half excited. Peter didn't seem to be scared at all, which made him feel a whole lot better. He held his breath while Peter smoothed out the paper.

"The Rat Pack are running," read Peter, by the torch light. "New rats come to the vicarage garden, 2 pm tomorrow. Signed, King Rat."

"What does it mean?"

Peter read it through again, thoughtfully, before scrambling back into his sleeping-bag. "I think it's a gang. I saw some boys when I was out with Rusty, in the next street. They looked at me and said something to each other. I think it's them."

"Big boys?"

"Bigger than me – well, a bit bigger. I think they want me to join their gang."

Tom thought about this for a moment.

"Are you going to?"

"Yep."

"Aren't you scared?"

"Course not! Only little kids get scared."

Tom thought for a few more moments and then said, "I think I'll join too."

"They probably won't want you. It's a big boys' gang."

"They might. How do you know?"

"I just do. Now shut up and go to sleep."

Peter's voice was muffled. Tom lay down and thought some more, wondering what kind of gang

11

the Rat Pack could be. But before he'd decided, it was morning and light was streaming in across his face from the uncurtained window.

"Dad," said Peter at breakfast. "Where is the vicarage?"

They'd found some logs and kindling in the shed, built another fire and boiled a kettle and toasted bread for breakfast. They ate it sitting on rolled-up sleeping-bags and pillows, with plates and mugs on the floor beside them.

Tom gave a jump, and just missed spilling his tea. He'd almost thought that the tennis ball and the message of the night before had been a dream. He opened his mouth to say something, but Peter gave him a warning look and he closed it again.

"The vicarage?" asked Dad. "Well, the parish church is over there ..." He pointed to where the top of a steeple soared to the sky above the roofs, clearly seen from the window. "... so I suppose the vicarage is somewhere near there. Why do you ask?"

Peter took a bite of toast. "I just wondered."

He gave Tom another look, just to make sure. Tom felt a little tingle of excitement run down his backbone.

The van arrived mid-morning with the furniture and there was a great hustle and bustle of removal men and parents running up and down the stairs, arranging and rearranging. Children and dog were confined to the living-room, with two chests of books to arrange on the built-in shelves.

"To keep you from under our feet," said Dad.

The electricity was on, so it was warm despite the rather chilly, gloomy autumn day outside, and they were able to make beans on toast all round for lunch.

Afterwards Peter asked casually, "Is it all right if I go out for a bit?"

Mum nodded. "Take Tom with you. Emma and I will take a walk to the shops later on, when we're a bit straighter here."

The boys got into their jackets and Wellington boots. Tom felt another little shiver go down his backbone.

"We're going to the Rat Pack, aren't we?" he asked.

Peter just grunted. He seemed to be in a grumpy mood, but maybe he was just nervous. At any rate, he hadn't said that Tom wasn't allowed to come too.

It was quite cold once they had left the busy, untidy, cluttered warmth of the new house. Brown and yellow leaves were spinning down into the street from tall sycamores bordering the pavement. The days were getting shorter and winter was on its way. Both boys put their hands into their jacket pockets.

Peter was frowning, keeping his eyes on the church spire to guide them as they turned corners and walked along different streets. Tom was quite sure that they were lost. But suddenly they came out right next to the church, a tall, grey building with its steeple pointing into the grey autumn sky. Next to the church stood a large house, also grey, with a curl of blue smoke coming from its chimney and lots of windows just visible above a tangle of bushes, shrubs and trees in bright autumn colours in the large garden surrounding it.

They stopped at a gate, set between large overhanging rhododendrons. A sign on the gate said *The Vicarage*. This was it, all right.

Tom looked at Peter, who shifted from one foot to the other. "Is this it? Shall we go in?"

Peter hesitated. "I'm not sure."

Tom was peering through the gate into the green, tangled dimness of the shrubs beyond. His heart beat faster. "Let's go in, Peter. Are you scared?"

Peter's shoulders squared. "Course not. Only little kids get scared. I'm just wondering if the gate's locked."

Tom tried the gate. It wasn't locked. He undid the latch and pushed it open.

Chapter three
The Rat Pack

The vicarage garden smelt of damp earth and greenery. Several paths went off in different directions. There was the main one leading to the house, and several smaller ones pushing their way through the rhododendrons and lilacs. Peter and Tom stopped inside the gate, wondering what they should do next.

Next moment, a boy appeared from one of the smaller paths, making Tom jump. He was a bit bigger than Peter and had reddish hair and freckles. He said, "You're Peter, aren't you?"

Peter nodded. "How did you know my name?"

"We have our methods," said the boy mysteriously. He looked at Tom. "Who's this?"

"My brother," said Peter, sounding apologetic.

The red-haired boy looked rather doubtful. "We didn't expect you to come mob-handed."

Peter looked as though he didn't understand what this meant. Tom didn't know either, but he felt it had something to do with him being there. The boy said, "He's small, isn't he?"

"Yes," said Peter. "He's only eight."

"And a quarter," said Tom indignantly. He stood as tall as he could inside his Wellington boots.

"Well, I don't know." The red-haired boy rubbed his chin. "We'll have to ask the King Rat. He'll decide. Come on."

He turned and led the way along one of the small paths, pushing aside the branches of dark green, glossy leaves.

The paths twisted and turned, but came out at last into a kind of clearing, with a shed or hut in the middle of it. Around the doorway, sitting on an old upturned wheelbarrow and a broken garden seat, or leaning against the wall, were three other boys, all bigger than Peter.

The red-haired boy marched up to the one standing near the shed door. "Here he is, Sir. He came."

"So I see." The King Rat folded his arms and frowned at them. He didn't look much like a king. For one thing, he was the smallest of them, though still taller than Peter. He had dark wavy hair and glasses, and his jeans had holes in both knees. Everyone else was quiet as he looked at Peter and Tom, sizing them up.

"Hmm," he said at last in a thoughtful way. Then he added, "Do you wish to join the Rat Pack?"

Peter nodded, his eyes bright, nervousness forgotten.

"Oh yes! Please!"

"Yes please," added Tom.

The King Rat ignored Tom, speaking to Peter. "You'll have to swear allegiance to the Pack. Loyalty for ever, and death to our enemies. Especially those Wildcats."

"Yes!" said Peter. Then he added, "Who are they?"

"Thieves and villains," said the King Rat. "Mindless morons. Lawless rabble. The scum of the earth."

"Especially that Big Jo," said the red-haired boy.

"They want to pinch our shed," said the fair-haired boy.

"Flippin' nerve!" said another.

Suddenly the Rats were all jabbering at once, waving their arms about and threatening terrible tortures when they got hold of the Wildcats.

"Silence!" thundered the King Rat, and there was quiet again. "Right," he said to Peter. "You'll do. There's more of them than us, and we needed someone else." He pointed to the red-haired boy, and then the others one by one. "That's Ian, and that's Baz, and that's Spike. You can call me Sir. You're in."

"Thanks!" Peter's eyes were brighter than ever.

"Thanks!" echoed Tom.

The King Rat seemed to see Tom for the first time. "I don't know about him, though. Does he follow you about everywhere?"

"He does usually," said Peter. He moved a step or two away from Tom. Tom moved up as well, staying close to Peter.

"Hmm," said the King Rat thoughtfully. Then he said, "I know. I've thought of something for him. Something special."

"He won't get hurt, will he?" asked Peter quickly.

"Course not." The King Rat beckoned to Ian, the red-haired boy, and whispered in his ear. The boy nodded. "You come with me," he said to Tom.

Tom looked at Peter. For a moment, he thought he ought to stay with Peter, but Ian was saying,

17

"Come on, this way," and waiting for him to follow. When he looked back, Peter was already in the middle of the group, listening to them explaining about their plans to outwit the Wildcats.

He wondered what his own special thing was going to be. Ian walked fast, and he had to trot to keep up, but he asked breathlessly, "Where are we going? What will I have to do?"

"You'll see," said Ian.

They had left the vicarage garden behind and were out on the pavement again, up one street, round a corner, past a row of park railings and into another street. Dead brown leaves rustled under their feet and drifted into drive gateways. They seemed to be going an awfully long way, and Tom had no idea where they were at all. He puffed a little and tried to keep up with Ian's long strides.

They turned the corner into yet another street. A removal van stood outside one of the front doors. It looked somehow familiar.

"Ian," said Tom. "I think this is where— "

Ian was already running up the steps to the front door and pressing the doorbell. Then he said, "See ya!" and went off at a run, leaving Tom standing on the steps staring after him.

Tom might have run after Ian, but Dad had already answered the door, with an electric drill in one hand.

"Oh, it's you. Peter not back, then?"

Tom shook his head and went inside, blinking hard. He'd been nicely fooled.

It was warm inside, and smelt of mushroom soup. Mum was arranging pictures on the dining-room walls, telling Dad where to drill the holes.

The removal men were having a cup of tea in the

kitchen and Emma was sitting on the stairs singing to a row of dolls and teddies lined up on the step above. She turned round and looked at Tom. "Why are you crying?" she asked.

Before Tom could say anything the telephone rang and Mum answered it. She chattered away for a minute or two and then called out, "Tom, would you like a word with Grandma?"

Grandma's voice at the end of the phone sounded just the same as ever, warm and comforting. She said, "Hello, darling! How are you?"

Tom opened his mouth to speak, but his voice came out sounding hoarse and funny. Grandma said "Tom, are you all right? You sound a bit strange."

Tom cleared his throat. "I'm all right, Gran," he managed to say. He wished she was there with them, with her white cottonwool hair and comfortable lap that was just the place for a cuddle when things went wrong. Then she'd have given him a slice of bread and butter and her own home-made gooseberry jam, and sat down with him to watch TV for a bit. He'd soon have felt better. He wished they were back in the old house, just round the corner from Grandma's.

Gran was not easily fooled, even from far away. She said, "What's the matter, Tom? Don't you like the new house?"

It was no use fibbing to Gran, and he didn't try. He said, "Not much. I liked the old one better. I miss you, Gran. And I miss Kevin and Brian. I don't like the boys round here, much."

Chapter four
The Vicar's daughter

All that evening, and next morning, Peter was mysterious. Whenever Tom asked him anything about the Rat Pack, or what they were planning to do, or why they'd been so mean to him, Peter said, "Shut up!" or, "I'm not telling you!" or, "Go away and stop pestering me!"

In the end, he thumped Tom, and Tom rubbed his shoulder and said, "I'll tell Mum on you."

Peter said, "Go on, then! Tell her. Tell-tale!"

Tom felt his lips quiver, and turned away before Peter called him a cry-baby as well. Peter and he were friends usually, and it was mean of Peter to have secrets from him.

He didn't tell, but felt that he had to relieve his feelings somehow, so picked up Emma's favourite rag doll and kicked it around the room for a while. Of course Emma screamed, and Mum came rushing in and said that she didn't know what was the matter with them all, and that it would be a good thing when half term ended and they could all start their new schools.

In the afternoon Peter put on his boots and jacket and said he was going out for a while. Tom knew he was going to the Rat Pack. He grabbed his own boots and started climbing into them. Peter scowled at him. "Where d'you think you're going?"

"I'm coming with you."

"No, you're not."

"I am."

Peter sighed. "Look, you're not old enough to do things with me. Why don't you play with Emma? She's more your age."

Tom's mouth fell open at the unfairness of it. He was much nearer Peter's age than Emma's. While he was still thinking of how to reply, Peter was gone with a slam of the door and a rush of cold air, and his footsteps were thudding away down the steps.

Tom was left sitting on the stairs with one boot on and the other off. Peter didn't want him, not any more, not now that he'd joined the Rat Pack. It wasn't fair. It was mean. He picked resentfully at a bit of loose paint on the banister rail. It was a horrid beige colour. The whole house was horrid, and he wished they'd never come here.

He was watching TV with Emma a little later, when a knock came at the door. Mum answered it. She came back into the room looking rather puzzled.

"Tom, there's a girl here asking if you'd like to go and play."

Tom felt his eyes grow round with surprise. "A girl? Are you sure?"

"I think I can tell the difference," said Mum, who was tired and rather short-tempered with the upheaval of moving and the quarrelsome mood of her children. "She's a big girl – much older than you. She says she's the Vicar's daughter, but I think I'd better ask her in and find out more."

It was definitely a girl who followed Mum into the room, a *very* big girl - maybe eleven or twelve – but as tall as Mum, with large feet in Doc Marten's, tough jeans, a thick check lumberjack shirt and hair tucked up inside a peaked baseball cap. Round her waist was a wide leather belt with keys and a pocket knife and other things dangling from it. She had a big, booming voice too, and didn't seem at all shy. When she saw Tom, she called out, "Oh, hello! You must be Tom. I wondered if you'd like to come and play at my house for a bit."

Tom wasn't sure. He scrambled to his feet and looked at Mum for help. Emma put her finger in her mouth and stared at the big girl.

"That's really very kind of you," said Mum. "Are you from St John's vicarage?"

The girl nodded and fumbled in the back pocket of her jeans. "Nearly forgot. I was asked to deliver this to you as well. It's our parish magazine. There's a letter from my father, too. He sends one to everyone that's new here."

She handed over some rather crushed and crumpled papers, which Mum took and smoothed out and read. Tom noticed that the little doubtful frown had gone from Mum's forehead by the time she finished reading. Mum turned and smiled encouragingly at both the girl and himself.

"That really is kind of you," she said again. "Yes, I'm sure Tom would like to come and play. Our older boy Peter seems to be making new friends and Tom's feeling a bit left out. Shall we come to fetch him back in an hour or so? It'll be dark by then."

"Don't worry," said the girl. "I'll see he gets

home all right."

"Thank you," said Mum. "I really think we're going to like living here. It's nice and quiet, and everyone's friendly and seems to take an interest in each other. Well, hurry up, Tom, and get your things on."

There was nothing for it but to put on his outdoor things and go off with this strange, large, loud-voiced girl.

"I didn't quite catch your name," said Mum as they set off.

"Joanna," said the girl. "Joanna Southcott." She walked with long strides, and Tom had to break into a trot every now and then to keep up.

"Are you really from the vicarage?" he asked, with Peter and the Rat Pack still very much on his mind.

"'Course," said Joanna. "My dad's the vicar, Reverend Southcott. Do you go to church?"

"I don't know," said Tom. "I used to with Gran, sometimes. But Gran stayed behind when we moved."

"You should come to St John's," the girl told him firmly. Tom decided that she was probably a very bossy person. He wondered whether she knew that the Rat Pack met in her garden, and what she'd say if she found out. For a moment he thought of telling her. If they got into trouble for trespassing it would serve them right for being mean. Half of him quite liked the idea of Peter getting a good telling-off, but the other half remembered that Peter was his brother and they'd always been friends.

He was still considering the idea when the girl said, "I suppose you're wondering why I called for you."

Tom had been wondering this, in between the other thoughts. She was such a very tall girl, and he was small for his age and hardly reached her shoulder. Big girls and younger boys usually didn't hang around together, at least, not from choice.

They turned a corner into Church Street, where the spire of St John's reached up into the darkening sky. Without waiting for an answer, the Vicar's daughter said, "It's because you're small, you see. We've got something special that only a small person can do."

Tom stopped in the middle of the pavement, staring at her.

That's what the King Rat had said yesterday. Something special, he'd said. And it had all been a trick.

Was this a trick too?

The big girl paused impatiently and looked at him. "Come on. What have you stopped for?"

Tom tried to keep his voice from wobbling. "I don't want to come."

"Why not?"

Horrible suspicions were going round and round in Tom's mind. Maybe she wasn't the Vicar's daughter at all. Maybe this was all a trick to get him to the vicarage grounds where the Rat pack met. Maybe something awful was going to happen. Maybe she was one of the Rat Pack herself.

He'd forgotten that Peter belonged to the Rat Pack and that yesterday he'd desperately wanted to belong too. He gave a kind of gulp and turned to run for home.

But the big girl was quick on her feet and

grabbed him by the arm. He struggled to escape but she had a grip of steel.

"Listen, listen," she was saying, but he kept struggling until he had to stop for breath.

"Listen," she said again, still holding him tight, and squatting down on her heels so that she could look into his face. He saw that her eyes looked deep blue in the gathering dusk, and that her fringe under the peak of her cap was honey-coloured.

"Calm down!" she said firmly, and, strangely enough, he did. "Now," she said. "In case you're wondering, I know all about your brother joining those Rats. I know what they did to you yesterday. They're a sneaky lot. But they're not as clever as all that. There's not one of them that wouldn't squeal if I got hold of him and twisted his arm round."

Rubbing his own arm where she had been holding him, Tom could quite believe that. But, strangely, he wasn't afraid any more. Something about the girl's steady blue eyes and the sprinkling of honey-coloured freckles across her nose made him feel suddenly quite safe.

"OK," he said. "I'll come with you. What did you say your name was?"

"Joanna," said the girl. "Joanna Southcott. They call me Big Jo. I'm the leader of the Wildcats."

Chapter five

The Wildcats

"Where are we going?" asked Tom. "Are we nearly there?"

"Yes," said Joanna. They seemed to have been walking for a long time, and Tom was sure they'd already reached the vicarage gate and passed it. They now seemed to be walking round a thick hedge that had the vast looming bulk of St John's church enclosed inside.

The big girl paused at last beside the hedge. She dived into the thick laurels and parted the leaves, holding them back for Tom. He scrambled through the small gap.

"Where are we?"

"My garden. Private back entrance. We always use this way so those Rats don't see when we come and go."

Tom shivered. The huge church and adjoining vicarage cast enormous black shadows. It was almost dark now, and the bushes and tall trees in the vicarage garden seemed full of whispering secrets. He wondered whether, even now, the Rats, with Peter among them, were meeting at the shed in the middle of the great dark shrubbery at the other end of the garden.

He jumped suddenly. A cat had miaowed right there beside him. Then he saw that it was Joanna. She miaowed again, a long drawn-out yowl, her hands cupped round her mouth, and there was an answering yowl from somewhere not far away.

"Come on," said Joanna, and grabbed his hand. They ran across grass and dead brown fallen leaves and arrived breathless at the door of a little round summer-house under a spreading elm tree that suddenly appeared through the dusk. Next moment he had been pulled through the door and stood inside, blinking.

The summer-house was bright and colourful, though a little shabby and dusty. There was an elegant white metal table with matching chairs, padded garden seats and pretty curtains at the window. The curtains were drawn, and there was Calor gas for heat and light. Faces stared at Tom, faces which belonged to people sitting on the chairs. Suddenly feeling shy, he took refuge behind Joanna.

"You got him!" said a triumphant voice.

"And he's ever so small!" said another, sounding very pleased about it.

Tom began to wish he hadn't come after all. He looked at the others from the shelter of Joanna's large figure. There were four other Wildcats, and they were all girls. All of them were much bigger than him, it was true. A couple of them got up and peered closely at him.

"Oh good, he's really skinny," said a dark-haired girl.

"But he looks quite tough," said another.

"Are you good at climbing?" asked another.

Tom looked from one strange face to another.

He opened his mouth to say that he could climb quite well, but Big Jo was taking charge of the situation. She pulled up one of the white metal chairs and sat Tom firmly upon it.

"Shut up, you lot. Give him time to get used to us. Where's your manners? Have we got something to eat or drink that we could offer him?"

One of the girls pointed out that Big Jo had finished the last can of Coke and bag of crisps before she went to fetch Tom. But after some rummaging about, another one found half a stick of pink seaside rock and pressed it into his hand. He licked it, his legs dangling from the chair, his eyes moving from one to another.

"Now then," said Jo. "Let's get down to business. Tom, we are the Wildcats. This is Katie, and Kelly, and Sam, and that's Helen. Me you know. As you'll have gathered, I'm the leader. This horrible place is where we have to meet at the moment."

Tom licked the rock again, looking round at the summery room. He thought it was really quite nice. There were even pink geraniums in tubs and rows of little cuttings in pots on the window sills.

"We shouldn't be here really," said Joanna. "It's my Dad's summer-house. The church ladies have tea in here sometimes. My Dad doesn't like us hanging around in here. And we don't like it ourselves, but we have to make do, because our proper headquarters has been pinched."

"By those stinkers," said Katie – or was it Kelly?

"Sewer rats!" said Sam.

"Is that nice rock?" asked Helen.

Tom nodded. He bit off a piece and felt it bulging in his cheek.

"It came from Great Yarmouth," said Helen.

"Never mind the rock," said Joanna. She sat down on the chair opposite and leant forward, her elbows on her knees.

"The situation is this. Those Rats – may their socks rot – have taken over the shed, our shed. We have a plan to get it back. Only we need you to help us, Tom."

Tom felt his eyes grow as round as his bulging cheek. However could he help? What could they want him to do? He wanted to ask if it would be dangerous, and why Joanna's parents let the Rats play in their garden anyway, and whether they knew about Peter. But he didn't dare, and besides, the big lump of rock stopped him speaking at all.

"You see," Joanna went on, "they think they've got it all sussed out. They lock the shed and keep the key with them. That King Rat takes it when they go away, so we can't get in and take the shed back. But we're going to, all the same."

Tom chewed and swallowed and found his voice at last.

"Are you going to fight them?"

Jo shook her head. "No. Not that we couldn't wallop the lot of them, no trouble. Chew them up and spit them out in little bits. But we're the Wildcats. Cunning creatures of the night. No one sees us come and go. We'll use stealth."

Her blue eyes sparkled. "There's something they don't know. There's a spare key to the shed. On the second shelf, halfway along, under the biggest flower pot. We only need to get it and get back into the shed when they're not there. Once we're in we can defend it, no problem."

"Only the window's too small to get in," said

29

Helen.

"Shut up," said Jo. "I'm doing the explaining. The shed window is really tiny. Too small for any of us to climb through. Only someone small and skinny could do it, easy. We'd push them in, they'd get the key and pass it out to us. You see what I mean?"

Tom did. His heart began to thump hard against his ribs. He knew who the small skinny person was, and why he'd been brought here. A circle of eager faces was waiting to see if he would agree to the plan.

"Well?" asked Big Jo. "Will you do it?"

Chapter six
The rocket

Tom thought for a moment, while he carefully wrapped what was left of the pink rock in its sticky paper and put it down on the white metal table. He thought how mean it was that the Rats had taken what rightly belonged to the Wildcats. He thought about the Rats, and the horrid trick they had played on him. He thought about Peter, and how Peter didn't want him any more now that he had joined the Rats. In spite of her bossiness, he couldn't help liking Jo. The other Wildcats seemed quite nice too, when you began to get used to them. He said "Yes, I'll do it. I'll help you."

Jo gave him a slap on the shoulder with her large hand. "Good man! I knew you would! Right, let's make a plan."

"Are we going to do it now?" asked Kelly – or was it Katie?

"No time like the present!" said Jo briskly. She looked at her watch. "We've got three quarters of an hour before I have to take Tom back to his Mum. Plenty of time. Now, if those Rats are in their shed – our shed – we'll have to get them out and away. Create a diversion."

Tom didn't know what a diversion was, but the others seemed to. "We could set off the burglar alarm," said someone, but Jo shook her head. "No, silly. Dad's in his study and he'd come running out. Then we'd all be in for it."

"I've got a firework," said Sam, the dark-haired girl. "A rocket. Really big. My uncle got it for me and I was saving it for Guy Fawkes night. But you can have it if you like."

Jo considered this offer, chin in hands. "That might work. A rocket makes a good swoosh when it goes off. We're not supposed to let off fireworks ourselves, but it's only one. It might do the trick. Have you got it with you?"

Sam hadn't, but she offered to run home for it. She must have lived quite near, because she was soon back, panting, with the rocket in a plastic bag. While she was away, Joanna darted across to the vicarage house and came back with matches and an empty milk bottle. The Wildcats began to look excited.

"We must be quiet about it," said Jo. "We'll let it off round the corner of the vegetable patch, by the blackcurrants. It's far enough away from the shrubbery. If we can get them searching round here it'll give us enough time to get Tom in and get that key."

They filed out of the warm summer-house. The cold air clutched at Tom's nose and ears and the grass was stiff with the first early frost. He stayed close to Jo as they scuttled round the big house, past a lighted window with drawn curtains and towards a vegetable garden near the side entrance.

Amongst the blackcurrant bushes, Jo set up the rocket in the milk bottle and took out a match.

"You others stay against the house walls. I'll join you when I've lit it. Then, when it goes off, dash for the shrubbery, take cover and wait for those rats to come wriggling out."

Tom shivered, and not only with cold. Jo lit the touch paper and joined them near the walls. They waited for the first fizzing sound, holding their breaths. Nothing happened.

"Blow!" said Jo. "It hasn't caught. It's gone out."

"Will you try again?" asked Sam.

"No. That's really dangerous. I'm not that stupid. Oh, bother! What shall we do now?"

For once she seemed at a loss. Then suddenly, after all, there was a crackle and a fizz from the rocket. They waited, expecting any moment that it would soar upward with a swoosh and a scream.

But it didn't. "Oh no!" groaned Jo. "The bottle's fallen over."

For a moment the rocket hissed and fizzed on the ground. Then it suddenly exploded into life, not shooting upward but scorching across the ground and through the bushes with a muffled swoosh and a smell of gunpowder. They saw sparks shooting close to the edge of the rhododendrons near the gate and then disappear into their depths. Some of the Wildcats gasped. It had all happened so quickly.

Seconds later, there were boys' voices shouting and dark figures bursting from the shrubbery.

"What was that?"

"What's going on?"

"Is it those stupid Wildcats messing around again?"

They milled around the edge of the shrubs, looking to see where the rocket had gone. The

Wildcats flattened themselves against the walls near the side entrance and held their breath. If only the Rats would go off searching for the rocket their plans might work even yet.

But they didn't. Instead, the door of the vicarage opened and a shaft of bright yellow light spilled out across the flagstones and the sparkly grass beyond. A man's voice said, "Joanna? Are you there? What was that noise?"

Tom saw that the Rats had melted into the shrubbery again like silent shadows. He felt his toes curling inside his boots. Would the man see them there against the wall? Should they run for it?

To his surprise, Joanna stepped forward into the light.

"It's all right, Dad. I let off a rocket, that's all."

The others listened to the voices of Joanna and the man talking in the open doorway. They could tell that her dad was cross and that she was getting a telling-off. They watched Joanna's tall, sturdy silhouette, and the man's thinner and even taller silhouette, moving about in the light from the porch.

Joanna was being ordered inside, but her voice took on a pleading tone. Suddenly the door closed, and then Joanna was beside them again, breathless and urgent. "I've got to go in. Dad's in a terrible stew about me messing round with fireworks. He's probably right. Sorry. Afraid we failed that time. But we'll try again, something different. Come on, Tom, I'll take you home. We'll have to run all the way. I got Dad to give me a few minutes to tidy up the summer-house, and make sure everything's switched off. Then it's early bedtime for me, I'm afraid. No TV, and no supper either if I'm not careful."

Chapter seven
Tom and Peter

Tom was having his own supper in front of the TV set when Peter came in. Emma was already in bed and Mum and Dad were upstairs, fixing shower curtains, so there was just him and Rusty, leaning comfortably against each other and sharing the chocolate biscuits.

Peter's face was red from the cold and his grey eyes were bright. His curly brown hair was tangled as though he'd been running. He kicked off his boots into a corner, threw his jacket in a heap and came to warm his cold hands and feet in front of the fire. He tried to help himself to a chocolate biscuit but Tom was too quick for him and took the last one himself.

"Not still sulking, are you?" asked Peter.

"No," said Tom.

"What have you been doing?"

"Not much."

Tom could see that his brother was bursting to tell him what he'd been doing himself, and also that he wanted to be friends with Tom again. Peter sat down on the rug beside Tom and Rusty.

"Look, Tom, I couldn't take you along this afternoon. The Rats is for older kids. It's too dangerous for somebody as little as you. You might get hurt, or frightened. Things happen with the Rats. Really sudden things. Like – like bombs going off."

"It wasn't a bomb."

Peter turned and stared at him.

"What did you say?"

"It wasn't a bomb. It was only a rocket that went sideways instead of up."

He saw that Peter's mouth had fallen open a little. "How do you know about that?"

Tom was beginning to enjoy himself. He grinned at the look of amazement on Peter's face. Peter gave him a small punch on the arm, not hard enough to hurt. "How did you know? Tell me!"

"I was there."

"In the vicarage garden? You were not!"

"I was. Or how would I know about the rocket?"

Peter had no answer to that. He hugged his knees for a moment and then asked, "Did you follow me?"

"No."

Tom intended to keep Peter guessing for a long time, to serve him right, but just then Mum came clattering downstairs into the room.

"Oh, hello, Peter. I'm glad you're back. You're a bit late, you know."

"Sorry," said Peter. "I forgot the time."

"Well, remember another time. I must be able to rely on you. That Joanna Southcott brought Tom home exactly on the dot. A nice girl, that. And responsible with it. Do you want a hot drink, Peter?"

"No thanks," said Peter weakly, "I had some lemonade."

"Well, I'll fill your hot-water bottles then."

Tom looked sideways at Peter when Mum had left the room. Peter was looking rather put out. He said, "So you've wormed your way in with that Big Jo, have you?"

"No," said Tom. "I never wormed in at all. It was her idea."

"And I suppose you've gone and joined those Wildcats?"

Tom wasn't sure that he had. None of the Wildcats had actually said that he could join, or asked if he wanted to. But they needed him to have another try at getting the key of the shed, so that must mean he was a part of the gang now. He said, "Yes. I have joined the Wildcats."

Peter's expression grew grimmer. He was silent for a moment and then said, "I think that's really stupid."

"It's not," said Tom. "Anyway, you wouldn't let me join the Rats."

"It wasn't me. It was the others. Anyway, I told you, it's because you're too little."

"I'm not too little for the Wildcats. They like me little."

"They're a bunch of girls!"

"It doesn't matter. They're nice."

"Huh! Bunch of big girls! What do they do, play with dolls or something?"

"Lots of things," said Tom mysteriously. "But I'm not telling."

"As if I want to know! Stupid girls!"

All the same, he was cross enough to give Tom another thump, and this time it was hard enough to hurt. Tom thumped back, they rolled over together on the rug and the remains of Tom's hot chocolate got spilt on the carpet.

Mum came in with the hot-water bottles. She didn't notice the spill, because it was the same pale brown colour as the carpet, and Rusty had already licked most of it up. But she couldn't help seeing that they were fighting again. She ordered them both to bed at once.

Tom's dreams were full of exciting things, like fireworks soaring into dark skies and strange people leaping from small windows and chasing him through the bushes. He woke in a panic and lay listening to Peter's faint snores from the other bed. He was glad Peter was there, even if he was one of the Rats. He suddenly felt worried, though, about the thing he had to do himself: climb in through a small shed window, all by himself, and find the spare key. The longer he thought about it, the harder it seemed. What if he got stuck halfway? What if the Rats came back and caught him? What if he got trapped inside the shed and couldn't get out? He wished he could tell Peter about it, but he knew he couldn't. He was a Wildcat now, and Peter was a Rat, on opposite sides.

Just the same, it was very lonely. He did what he usually did when he woke after a bad dream, climbed out of his bed and went over to Peter's. Peter snorted and groaned, which he always did when this happened, but he moved over and made room for Tom.

"What's up? A nightmare?" he asked groggily.

"Sort of," said Tom.

"Never mind," muttered Peter. "Only a dream." And he was asleep again.

A big brother was always comforting to have, even one from another gang. Tom felt better right away, and it was morning before he knew it.

Chapter eight
Bad news

Everyone slept late next morning, except Emma, who got up early and decided to unpack all the crockery and kitchen things still in boxes and put them away on the shelves and in the cupboards. She also thought that while she was at it, it would be a good idea to draw pictures in green and orange crayon on the plain white kitchen walls.

Mum and Dad were not pleased. Emma had managed to break a cereal bowl and two cups, and the shelves and cupboards had not yet been scrubbed, so everything had to be taken out again. Also, they did not share her ideas about the decoration of the walls, so all the crayon had to be scrubbed off. That was the boys' job, and it took them all morning, which they thought was very unfair.

At lunch time there was a phone call from Mrs Baines, who lived next door to Grandma. Mum called Dad to the phone and they both talked for a while. Peter and Tom both wanted to talk to Grandma, but Mum said they couldn't.

"Grandma's not well," she said. "She won't feel like talking."

Tom thought of the times Grandma had been ill

before, when she'd tripped on some steps and hurt her ankle, and when she'd had bronchitis. Then she'd sat with her feet propped on a stool by the fire, with a blanket tucked cosily round her. Mum had taken in her meals on a covered plate, and the boys had fetched and carried and run errands for her. They wouldn't be able to do that now, with Grandma so far away.

"Mum," said Tom. "Who will look after Grandma while she's ill?"

"Mrs Baines is taking care of her," said Mum, "and the people from the church will help too."

Tom remembered that the people from Grandma's church had helped last time. But he still felt worried. A horrid sick feeling had come into his stomach and he decided that he didn't want a second helping of ice-cream after all.

Dad was a bit cross to find that there were a lot of holes in the dining room walls that hadn't been properly filled in by the people who'd lived there before. He mixed some paste from a bag of white powder and filled some of them, but the white stuff was soon finished. "I'm out of filler," he said. "Anyone going to the shops?"

"I'll go," said Peter quickly.

"I'll go as well," said Tom. Peter frowned at him.

"You don't have to tag along."

"I'm not tagging along. I'd just like to go to the shops."

"Well, you can't come with me."

"Why not?"

"Because you can play with Emma. Or those silly Wildcat girls."

Peter might be kind when one was scared in the night, but he'd gone back to being mean again now. Tom thought that it might be rather nice to see Joanna again. He felt much braver in the daylight.

He said, "All right, then. I'll go and see the Wildcats."

Peter seemed to change his mind. "You can't. You're not allowed, all by yourself."

"I am."

"Not."

"Am."

Dad came in with the list of odds and ends they needed from the decorator's shop. "Quarrelling again! What's got into you two? Here you are, Peter. Don't take too long."

Peter gave Tom a last glare as he disappeared into the hall to get his outdoor things.

"Mum," said Tom. "Can I go too?"

Mum had her sleeves rolled up and was scrubbing kitchen shelves. She said, "Yes, if you stay with Peter. Don't go wandering off on your own. Okay?"

"Okay."

But by the time Tom reached the front door there was no sign of Peter. Peter's bike was gone, and he was probably already half-way to the shops.

Tom was strictly forbidden to take his own bike out by himself. He hesitated in the doorway. "Close the door behind you!" called Mum. "There's a terrible draught going right through. And stay with Peter, mind. Promise?"

"Yes Mum."

Tom closed the door behind him with a strange feeling in his stomach. He never told fibs to Mum as a rule. But he'd done it now. Mum thought he was with Peter, and he'd let her think so, which was just the same.

But somehow, he was reluctant to go back inside and tell her what had really happened. They were too busy to bother with him, anyway. If they'd still been at home, he'd have gone round to Gran's for a bit. She might have been sweeping up the autumn leaves in her back garden and having a bonfire. Then they'd have lit a fire inside and made toast and hot chocolate, just the two of them and Pickle. He felt tears prick at the backs of his eyes. Gran's house and Gran and Pickle were far away. And Gran was ill, too ill even to speak to him on the phone.

Suddenly, he wanted desperately to see Gran. Mum and Dad should have got in the car straight away and driven back to look after her. But all they cared about was the stupid new house. And all Peter cared about was the Rat Pack.

Well, *he* cared about Gran. He wouldn't mind going back and taking care of her. In fact, maybe he'd do just that. He felt his heart give a sudden little jump. He could catch a bus himself and go back to Gran's. He knew the name of her town, the town he'd lived in himself for eight and a quarter years. He didn't know where he'd catch a bus though. But there'd surely be someone he could ask, a policeman or a traffic warden.

He looked at the closed front door behind him. Gran would be pleased to see him, he was sure. Quickly, before he changed his mind, he walked down the steps and out into the street.

Chapter nine
Tom alone

He felt strange, and very small, being out in the street all by himself. At the corner of the road Tom turned and looked back, to see if he could still pick out his own front door. The only way he could tell was by its colour, and even then he wasn't sure, because one or two others were almost the same. For a moment he wanted to run back and find the right door, and get back inside where it was warm and safe. But he remembered Gran, and squared his shoulders, and turned the corner.

He thought he'd keep walking until he saw someone grown-up and important-looking, someone in uniform, a policeman or a traffic warden. Then he'd ask the way to the bus station.

It was a crisp, clear day. Most of the trees had changed the colours of their leaves now, and fallen ones lay in drifts along the gutters. There was a smell of bonfires in the air. A horse chestnut tree hung over a wall beside the road, and some children his size were looking for conkers under it. Tom felt his footsteps slow for a moment, thinking longingly of smooth, shiny, dark brown conkers. One of the children looked at him and smiled in a friendly way, but Tom frowned and began to walk fast again. He had more serious things to think about than conkers.

He noticed for the first time that the town sloped downhill in every direction, the streets leading to the cluster of huddled roofs and buildings that was the centre. The tall spire of St John's poked up from somewhere in the middle of it. The houses were different to the ones in the old town too, mostly grey stone instead of red brick, with dark slate roofs. The people were friendly, looking at him in an interested way and sometimes calling a greeting. He didn't answer any of them. He'd been taught never to speak to strangers.

There seemed to be no policemen about anywhere. Tom felt his steps growing slower again. Maybe it hadn't been such a good idea after all. Maybe there wouldn't be a bus going to Grandma's town, even if he found the bus station. Maybe it would cost an awful lot of money, and he wouldn't have enough.

He stopped suddenly, right in the middle of the pavement, colliding with a plump lady walking along with a shopping trolley. She put out a hand to steady him. She had hair like Grandma's and didn't seem to mind the collision too much. She smiled and said, "All right, love?"

"Yes, thank you," said Tom, a little breathlessly. He'd suddenly remembered that he hadn't any money at all. He hadn't thought of it until now. He couldn't go on a bus without money. He'd have to give up the idea of going to Grandma's. He might as well just go home to tea.

It was quite a relief, really. Tom turned and began to walk back the way he had come, up the gently sloping street, while the lady with the trolley went on towards the shops. But at the top of the hill he found he couldn't quite remember the next bit. Had he turned right or left here? He looked back towards the town centre again. There was the spire of St John's sticking up from the houses and shops, the only place he really recognised. Apart from that, he really hadn't a clue where he was.

Tom stood at the corner of the road, feeling very small and lonely. It wasn't very busy here, halfway through the afternoon on a working day. Some cars went past. Then a boy in a blue cycling helmet went by on a bike, head down, riding fast downhill. He turned and looked at Tom as he passed. At the bottom of the hill, he made a wide curve and then came up again, slowing down as he reached Tom.

"You lost, or something?"

Tom shook his head. He wasn't lost, not really. Or was he?

"What's the matter, then?"

Tom didn't know what to say. He blinked hard and tried to look as though he knew exactly where he was going next. The boy took one foot off the pedal and rested it on the pavement.

He was about Peter's size, or a bit bigger, and had a scarf wrapped round his face so that only a pair of eyes behind glasses showed under the blue helmet. There was something vaguely familiar about him, though Tom didn't know what.

"Where do you live, then?" asked the boy.

Suddenly, Tom found he couldn't remember his new address at all. He had a feeling that it was something to do with trees. Was it Elm Street? Oak

Road? And what on earth was the house number?

The boy was watching him, holding the handlebars with hands in yellow and blue cycling gloves.

"Tell you what," he said, his voice muffled in the scarf.

"If you're lost, the place to go is the vicarage. The Vicar knows everybody. He'll soon sort you out. I'm going along that way myself. I'll take you, if you like."

Tom let out his breath, though he hadn't known he'd been holding it. Jo would be at the vicarage. She'd be able to point him in the right direction. Suddenly he wanted to see Jo very much indeed.

"Yes please," he said with relief.

The boy got off his bike and wheeled it, walking along beside Tom at a slow pace to suit Tom's shorter legs. He didn't say much and kept his face well wrapped in the scarf. Tom didn't say much either. He still felt quite near to crying and didn't want to take the risk. They walked down the hill together, turning corners until suddenly there was St John's Church and the vicarage right in front of them.

"There you are," said the boy in the blue helmet. "Just go up and knock on the door. There's a light on inside."

Tom was feeling much better. It was funny how comforting the sight of a familiar place could be. In the vicarage garden the shrubbery lay quiet, bright with autumn colours of gold and brown and russet. He wondered if Peter and the Rat Pack were meeting there at this very moment.

He turned to say thank you, but the boy was back on his bike, speeding away on the road bordering the vicarage garden. Tom gazed after him for a moment, wondering where he'd seen him before. It was the voice that sounded most familiar, even though the boy had mumbled into the scarf – it was almost as though he didn't want to be recognised.

If Tom hadn't known beyond doubt that the Rat Pack was a gang of villains, thieves and liars, never known to be kind to anyone, he'd almost have said that the boy on the bike sounded like the King Rat himself.

Chapter ten

Tea at the vicarage

Tom felt suddenly small and lonely again, walking up the vicarage path all by himself. It took all his courage to stand on tiptoe and lift the large brass door-knocker. It seemed to make a very loud knock. He hoped that it would be Jo who came to the door to answer it.

But it wasn't. Instead, a tall man in faded jeans and a blue sweatshirt came to the door. His sleeves were pushed up and he looked a bit like Dad when he was in the middle of his DIY and had been interrupted. Maybe the vicarage was being painted and decorated too.

He peered at Tom in a slightly puzzled way and said, "Oh, hello. I don't think I know you, do I?"

Tom felt a little nervous. He said, "I'm called Tom. Is Jo in, please?"

A loud blast of music came from upstairs as a door was opened. The tall man laughed. "She's in, all right! Joanna! Someone to see you!"

Joanna came thundering down the stairs in her Doc Martens and jeans, a baggy T-shirt and her peaked cap on back to front, various possessions dangling from her belt. She seemed pleased to see Tom. "Tom! I was just thinking of coming over to yours." She turned to introduce Tom and the tall man. "Dad, this is Tom. Tom, this is Dad."

"We've met," said her dad, but he shook hands with Tom just the same, and said, "Nice to meet you, Tom. I hope you'll excuse me," and disappeared into another room.

"He's ever so busy," said Jo. "Writing sermons and things. Come upstairs."

She turned and bounded up the stairs again, two steps at a time. Tom followed, still rather surprised to learn that the tall man was Jo's dad. So he must be the Vicar, even though he didn't look a bit like one and wasn't even wearing proper Vicar's clothes.

Tom thought Joanna's room was the messiest he'd ever seen. Piles of clothes, books, cassettes, magazines lay on the bed, the chairs and the floor. Cupboard doors stood ajar, and drawers were half-opened with things hanging out from them.

"Excuse the mess," said Jo. "I'm thinking of having a tidy-up one of these days. After I've fixed those Rats. You see, I happen to know they'll all be at Scouts tonight. When the Wildcats come over after tea, we can go and get that key."

"I have to be back quite soon," said Tom hurriedly. Then a thought struck him. "I wouldn't mind, I mean, couldn't I go and do it now, while it's light?"

"Oh, it's no fun in the daylight!" said Joanna. "After dark's the thing, creeping up with torches and barricading ourselves in, in case they decide to come round after Scouts. We might have a really good battle if they did!"

Tom was not so sure that he was ready for a battle yet. He said, "I have to go home for tea."

"Never mind. I'll pick you up later. Better still, let's ring up and ask if you can stay here to tea. What's your phone number?"

Dad had carefully taught Tom and Peter their new phone number, as well as their address. But he hesitated. He had the uneasy feeling that he shouldn't be here at all, and that there might be trouble to come.

"Can't you remember it?" asked Jo impatiently.

"Yes," said Tom with a sinking heart, and told her the number. Strangely enough, he could remember the address as well now, quite clearly: 24, Elm Street.

"Good," said Jo. "Let's go and ring straight away. No time like the present, I always say."

To Tom's surprise, Mum agreed to let him stay to tea at the vicarage. "She sounded a bit surprised," said Joanna. "Seemed to think your brother must be here too. But she said it was okay."

Tea was thick slices of bread spread with butter and strawberry jam, large slices of fruit cake, bananas, chocolate biscuits and apple juice, all served by Joanna at the big wooden table in the rambling vicarage kitchen. Her father didn't appear and her mother didn't seem to be about either. It was easy to see how Jo had grown so large, from the amount she ate. Bread, cake and fruit disappeared rapidly between her munching jaws. "Won't your Mum mind?" asked Tom, as Jo finished a jar of jam and started on one of lemon curd.

"I haven't got a Mum," said Jo, scooping out a spoonful. "I mean, I used to, of course, but she died when I was little. Mrs Smythe comes in to do the cooking and cleaning, but it's her day off today. She made this fruit cake. It's good isn't it? Have another slice? I'm going to."

Tom declined the cake. He swallowed some apple juice with a gulp. He'd never met anyone before whose mother had died. The thought gave him a funny feeling in his stomach and made him want to go home quickly and check on his own Mum.

He glanced sideways at Joanna, to see if it made her sad to talk about her mother. She looked the same as usual, he thought.

But he noticed that her hand went to her belt, where a small leather pouch hung among the keys and penknives. Her thumb stroked the worn brown leather, and for some strange reason Tom was reminded of an old baby blanket he'd carried around until he was five or six, and how the familiar feel and smell of it had comforted him when he was lonely or sad.

Joanna's voice, though, was as loud and cheerful as ever.

"Have you finished? Good! The others should be here at any moment. We'd better get over to the summer-house."

She piled the plates and mugs into the sink.

"I'll do them later."

The other Wildcats began to arrive at the summer-house as it grew dark. Katie had a tube of fruit gums and Sam a packet of toffees, which they shared between them as they made plans and waited for the time when all Rats would be safely at the Scout hut. Tom wondered what Peter would be doing. He was not quite old enough for Scouts and hadn't joined the Cubs here yet.

At last it was time for action. They took a small torch, put on coats and headed for the shrubbery. The frosty spell had given way to damper, milder weather and the greenery dripped a little. The garden shed stood dark and lonely in its clearing.

"Now," said Joanna. "Inside, there's an old table just under the window. We'll give you a bunk up and you can land on the table when you climb through. You can have the torch. Remember, the biggest flower pot on the second shelf."

Without more delay, Tom found himself hoisted up by several pairs of arms and raised to the level of the small glassless window. He put his head through and grasped the sill. The Wildcats pushed from behind. Tom would have liked to take a little more time about it, but they kept pushing until his body was half over the sill. He began to wish he'd eaten a little less tea, but with another push most of him was through and his hands were reaching down to touch the solid surface of the table inside. Next moment his legs and feet had somehow followed and he had landed in a heap on the table top. He gathered himself together and fumbled for the little torch in his pocket.

The shed looked very dusty and shadowy in the thin yellow beam of torch light. The only furniture was the old table, a few sagging chairs and a box or two. Shelves held garden tools and pots, old newspapers, dusty sacks and odds and ends. Old garden forks, rakes and spades leant against the walls. Tom thought that it wasn't half as nice as the bright, cheerful summer-house, and wondered why the Wildcats wanted it so much.

Whispered instructions came from outside.

"Tom! Get down from the table, climb on a box

and get the key from under the flower pot. Go on!"

The shed smelt as musty and dusty as it looked, Tom scrambled down and picked his way across to the shelf. The key was there all right, just where Jo said it would be. He picked it up with a sigh of relief.

"Got it?" hissed Jo from outside. "Good! Now then, pass it out to us. Better climb up again and hand it out. Don't throw it— "

Too late. In his eagerness to finish the job and escape from the dusty shed, Tom had already tossed the key towards the window space. It went through and landed somewhere on the ground outside, The Wildcats seemed to be searching for it, scrabbling around outside in the dark. "Oh, no! Where did it go? Tom, why didn't you wait? We can't see a thing. Tom, you'll have to give us the torch. Oh, blow it!"

Tom stood inside, heart thumping. The key was lost and he was still inside. He scrambled up onto the table top, scraping his knees, panic making his voice shaky and breathless. "Jo! Get me out of here!"

The others were too busy searching and complaining to pay him any attention. Then at last someone said, "Got it!" in tones of relief. There were sounds of a key grating in the lock and then the door was creaking open.

Tom scrambled down from the table, weak with relief. "What do we do now?" asked one of the Wildcats when they had all crowded into the dim shadowy shed.

"We wait a bit," said Jo. "Quietly, so we can ambush them if they come. Cheeky things! Look what it says there!"

She pointed the torch beam at a large notice on the wall, which said in big black letters: **This is the HQ of the Rat Pack. Rats for ever and down with the Wildcats!**

There was also a large plastic container with biscuits and sweets inside, and a half-full bottle of Coke.

"Shall we help ourselves?" asked Katie hopefully.

Jo looked tempted for a moment. Then she said, "Better not. It might be poisoned."

She prowled around, looking at a football, a skateboard and other odds and ends stowed away under the shelves.

Suddenly there was a noise from outside. Someone was coming, swishing and thudding along the shrubbery path.

"Torch out!" whispered Jo. "Quiet, everyone! Get ready to defend our property to the last breath!"

Chapter eleven
Captured!

Tom was rather confused about what happened next. Whatever it was, it happened very quickly. All of a sudden, boys were bursting into the shed, pushing, shouting, scuffling. Boxes were pushed aside and a pot crashed down from a shelf.

"Hey, they're in here, those Wildcats!"

"Cheek of it! Let's get 'em!"

"Chuck 'em out!"

There was a great deal more scuffling and shoving.

"Ouch! That hurt!" came Jo's voice. "Get off, James! We're here and we're staying! Why aren't you at Scouts, anyway?"

"Cancelled," said the King Rat's voice. "Scoutmaster's ill. You've got a nerve, coming in here! Hop it, go on!"

"No way!"

"Well, we'll use force, then!"

"You and whose army?"

Tom felt himself buffeted about among larger bodies as the Rats and Wildcats battled in the darkness. He could not tell which was which. A flailing elbow dug him in the ribs and someone trod heavily on his toes. More tools and pots were pushed about and fell over. He thought he recognised Peter among the Rats, but he wasn't sure.

Then, suddenly, the door had burst wide open and the whole struggling mob had spilled outside. He saw Jo trip over and sprawl winded on the grass. The King Rat stood over her in triumph.

"Now then! Give in, and get going!"

Jo picked herself up, breathless. "Oh, all right. We're going. For now. Come on, Cats. We'll get you lot another time."

Some of the Rats jeered and cat-called. The Wildcats were edging away along the path between the bushes, following their leader. Jo fired a parting shot.

"Good riddance, you scummy rodents! May your fangs fall out!" Her voice was growing fainter as she disappeared among the bushes. Then suddenly it bellowed out full blast. "We can get in anytime, because WE'VE GOT A KEY!"

"WHAT!" The King Rat was no longer gloating. "Get them, gang! Don't let them get away! Get that key back!"

But the Wildcats had already escaped, crashing and thudding among the shrubs and bushes, their footfalls growing fainter.

Tom tried to follow, but he was not quite fast enough to keep up. Suddenly a long pair of arms grabbed him from behind. He tried to fight but he was lifted bodily with his legs kicking in mid-air. Ian's voice said, "Ah! A prisoner! Or a hostage."

Tom was too surprised to yell. He struggled all the way back to the shed but was no match for several big Rats. They dumped him on an old chair and stood in a circle looking at him in the torch light. He saw that Peter was there, with a rather anxious look on his face.

"What are you going to do with him, Sir?" asked Spike.

The King Rat folded his arms. "Bargain. His life for the key. Good work, Ian, grabbing him like that."

"Thank you, Sir," said Ian.

"If they don't give back the key, what will you do to him?" asked Peter.

The King Rat didn't answer. He walked to and fro, arms folded, thinking. Tom trembled a little. He wondered if it was nearly time for him and Peter to go home.

The shed was a shambles, with furniture and pots and tools knocked over and lying about. Tom noticed suddenly that Jo's leather pouch lay on the floor, torn from her belt during the fight. Quickly he moved his foot to cover the pouch, hiding it from the Rats' view. The King Rat ordered Spike and Baz to tidy up. Then he said, peering at Tom, "He's a good fighter, for his size. What's his name? Tom, is it? Hey, Tom, how would you like to leave those girls and join the Rats?"

For a moment, Tom was tempted. It would be nice to be on the same side as Peter. Then he thought of Jo, and the piles of bread and butter and strawberry jam she'd given him for tea, and her golden freckles, and her kindness. He shook his head. The King Rat frowned.

"Hmm. Stubborn. Never mind, I preferred the hostage idea. Have they really got a key?"

Tom didn't answer. If he was to be called stubborn, he might as well act the part.

"You won't torture him, will you?" asked Peter anxiously.

Tom wished that Peter hadn't mentioned torture. He hadn't thought of it himself and maybe the King Rat hadn't either. He began to feel a little sick.

"No," said the King Rat. "We'll just use him as a pawn. Those Wildcats are sure to try and get him back. We'll have to take him to the dungeon."

Tom began to feel really alarmed. He found his voice. "I think we ought to go home soon."

No one took any notice.

"The dungeons, and then negotiations," said the King Rat. "I'm the one who says what happens around here. Rats, to the deepest dungeon with him!"

Tom was seized and pulled to his feet. He only just managed to snatch up Jo's leather pouch from the floor and stuff it into his jeans pocket. No one seemed to notice. Held firmly by the scruff of the neck, he was marched between damp, dark bushes towards the vicarage itself.

Peter hung back. "We can't go in there, can we? The Vicar lives there. What'll he say?"

"Who asked your opinion?" said the King Rat scornfully. "Just do as I say. I give the orders around here, remember?"

Peter said no more. Tom hoped with all his might that Jo would come galloping down the stairs and rescue him. But she didn't. He thought sadly that by now she and the other Wildcats were probably in the summer-house, licking their wounds. A line of light from beneath the study door showed that the Reverend Southcott was still busy in there.

"Quick!" said the King Rat. "Before someone comes!"

The Rats with their prisoner hurried across the hall and unfastened a door at the end. Tom stood at the top of a flight of stone steps, leading down into somewhere cold and dark. One of the Rats switched on his torch, pointing it down into the darkness. Tom found himself pushed forward onto the top step.

"To the dungeon!" said the King Rat.

Chapter twelve
In the dungeon

The dungeon was half full of coal, glistening black in piles of shiny lumps, or lying in dusty heaps. There was no window, just dark, dusty walls, a couple of coal shovels, a brass coal scuttle with a broken handle and a wooden coal box.

"Sit!" ordered the King Rat, and pushed Tom down upon the coal box. He turned the broken coal scuttle upside-down and sat upon it himself. The others had to remain standing, one of them holding the torch.

"Here you stay," said the King Rat, "until our enemies have met our demands. Now, let's plan negotiations."

There was a great deal of talk about how this should be done. The dungeon was unheated, and a cold chill came from the damp walls. One or two of the Rats began to complain of the cold, and that they were fed up of standing. Tom saw that Peter was shifting uneasily from one foot to the other.

"I'll write a ransom note," said the King Rat. "Setting out our terms. Anyone got a pen and paper?"

Someone found an old chocolate bar wrapper

and someone else had a ball-point refill in his pocket. The King Rat smoothed the paper and sat frowning as he thought what to write. It grew colder in the dungeon.

The note seemed to be taking a long time. Some of the Rats began to mutter to one another about supper and television programmes. They shuffled their feet and stirred up clouds of coal dust, which got up Tom's nose and made him sneeze. He wondered if the Vicar would try and rescue him if he shouted for help, but he didn't dare try.

Suddenly everyone stopped talking and listened, because a new noise had come from somewhere above. A slithering and scraping in one corner, of the coal cellar roof, followed by a rush of even colder air from outside. Then Joanna's voice.

"Hey, you, rat-face! I know you're there and I know you're holding one of us prisoner. You'd better let him go double-quick!"

The Wildcats had removed the outside cover of the coal-chute.

The Rats snarled in reply, forgetting their complaints in the hope of more action.

"Come and get him if you want him!"

"Yeah, come down here and see what you'll get!"

"We'll roll you in the coal dust!"

"Wait!" said the King Rat. "What we want is that key back. Let's negotiate. I was doing a note, but talking is better. Guard the prisoner, you lot. I'm going out."

"All right," said Joanna's voice. "But the rest of the Cats will come in. To make sure the prisoner's safe and properly treated, and no monkey business. I can't trust you lot."

It was agreed. With some puffing and grunting, the rest of the Wildcats dropped into the dungeon and slid and slithered down the pile of coal. The King Rat scrambled up it and heaved himself out. His and Jo's voices sounded faintly, deep in complicated discussion.

The remaining Wildcats and Rats looked at each other in the torch light. All of them were already covered with coal dust, more or less. Some of them looked very bored as well.

"They'll take ages," said Spike. "They always do."

"Shall we fight while we're waiting?" suggested Sam.

"No," said Ian. "You girls would mess up your hairstyles."

"Ha ha," said Kelly sarcastically.

"Won't we get into trouble with the Vicar?" asked Peter. "For being here?"

"No" said Ian. "We're allowed."

"They're cousins," said Katie.

"Joanna and James," said Ian. "James – I mean the King Rat – is allowed to play around the vicarage any time, and so are we."

Tom felt relieved somehow. The fact that Joanna and James were cousins was a great load off his mind in a curious way.

Helen was leaning forward towards Tom, peering at something through the gloom.

"Isn't that Jo's leather purse hanging out of your pocket?"

Tom felt his hand go protectively over the leather pouch.

"Yes. It fell off in the fight."

"You'd better be careful. She never lets anyone

touch that, not ever."

"No one knows what she keeps in it," said Katie.

"Let's have a look then," suggested Ian. "While she's busy. James is always trying to see what she keeps in it."

Tom felt his grip tighten. He stuffed the pouch further into his pocket. "No. I'm keeping it for Jo."

"You're scared. Scared of a big bossy girl!" said Spike scornfully.

Tom was silent. He was a bit scared, but not of Jo. And he wasn't letting anyone have her pouch, if he could help it.

For a moment he wondered what would happen if the Rats and Wildcats together decided to grab him and take the pouch away. But Kelly was speaking again.

"Jo does always like to be the boss," she said thoughtfully.

"Only James won't let her," said Ian. "Because she's a girl, and so big. They're the same age, though."

"She IS very bossy," said Katie. "No one else ever gets to choose anything. Or make any decisions."

"Nor do we," said Baz. "James always decides everything."

"I hate having to call him Sir," said Ian.

"They're always fighting over that silly shed," said Sam after a short pause. "And it's not really all that good a place. We get a lot of hassle for nothing, really."

There was silence for a moment as they all looked at one another in the dim torch light.

"We don't HAVE to do what they say," said Katie in a small voice.

"We could get out up the steps and go home, if we wanted to," said Baz.

"They couldn't stop us," said Spike.

Mutiny hung in the cold air along with the coal dust. The leather pouch in Tom's pocket was forgotten. He looked at the Wildcats and the Rats, all mixed up together and complaining about their leaders.

There were voices at the top of the chute, and then Joanna and James came down feet first in a great shower of dust. At once the Rats and Wildcats divided into their two separate groups and were quiet.

"Right!" said the King Rat. "It's agreed. They get the prisoner back, and we get the key."

"Can we go home then?" asked Peter.

"Yes," said the King Rat.

There was some digging about in the pockets of Jo's jeans, while she found the key and handed it over to the King Rat. Then she led the way up the steps, opened the door, looked around and beckoned them all to come out. Blinking in the bright light of the hallway, they emerged, a filthy, tousled, coal-blackened crowd.

"Oh my goodness!" said Jo. "What a sight! Let yourselves out, quick, before you're seen! Tom and Peter, I'll have to take you home just as you are. No time to clean up."

The departing Rats and Wildcats left a trail of black footprints from the coal dust across the hallway to the side door. The rest of them melted away, and Jo hurried Tom and Peter home through the cold dark streets. On the way, Tom handed her the leather pouch, and was rewarded by a slap on the back and, "Oh, good man, Tom. I thought I'd have to search for that later!" as she fastened it to her belt again.

Jo seemed in good mood altogether. Once or twice, they heard her give a quiet chuckle as they hurried along. Then, suddenly, she burst out with a great booming laugh.

"Oh, the idiots! The poor blind creatures. I've fooled them again."

Tom looked at her, smeared with coal-dust in the light of the orange street lamps.

"How do you mean?"

"The key!" spluttered Jo. "He thinks he's got the spare key. But I fooled him. That key is from the cupboard in the spare room!"

Chapter thirteen
Tom and the Vicar

Both Tom and Peter were sure that they would catch it from Mum when she saw the state they were in. She did let out a little shriek when she answered the door and saw them standing grimy and coal-blackened on the steps. Even Rusty gave a startled "woof" before he realised that it was just Tom and Peter. But after Mum had sent them to wash off the worst in the kitchen and had a talk with Jo, she seemed quite happy.

"Such a nice girl," she said. "I've never met a girl of that age quite so mature and responsible. And pleasant and polite with it. She's offered to have you both again tomorrow. It's a real help to have you out from under our feet while we're decorating. Though perhaps you ought to keep out of the coal cellar in future," she added, and shepherded them upstairs towards the bathroom.

"We'll have her round here to tea as soon as we're a bit straighter," she went on, running water into the bath. "You'd like that, wouldn't you?"

"Yes," said Tom.

"Bossy boots!" muttered Peter.

Peter stayed in a grumpy mood while they were getting undressed and getting into the bath. Tom thought it was because Jo had fooled the Rats, and he was right. He saw the glint in Peter's eye that meant Peter wouldn't mind having a fight. But it wasn't really possible to fight much in a bath full of hot slippery bubbles, except for splashing and drenching each other with huge tidal waves. The bath water soon turned grey, and there was a black tidemark round the bath when they got out.

In the morning, Mum phoned Mrs Baines to ask how Grandma was.

"Still rather poorly," she reported to the rest of the family. "This cold weather doesn't help. But Mrs Baines and the church people are taking good care of her."

Tom had almost forgotten how worried he had been about Grandma, with all the excitement of being captured by the Rats and imprisoned in the dungeon. But now all the worry came back with a rush. Last night, he'd meant to say his prayers and ask God to make Grandma well again. Grandma always told him he could ask God anything he wanted. But suddenly, just as he'd been about to ask, he'd remembered the big fib he'd told Mum that afternoon. He hadn't got into trouble about it because she hadn't found out. She still thought he'd been with Peter all the time. But somehow, he felt that he couldn't ask God for such an important favour after all.

When Joanna came to call for them later, Grandma was still on his mind. He thought about her all the way to Joanna's house, and when St John's church and vicarage came into view it gave him an idea. The church was God's house, and maybe, if he asked, the Vicar would take him there and help him to pray about Grandma.

But when he asked Jo if her father was in, his hopes were dashed. "Not at the moment. He had to go out. Someone died and he had to go and make the arrangements. Some old lady. He'll be in later."

Tom felt himself grow cold inside. An old lady had died! People did die, even people who weren't as old as all that, because Jo's mother had. But especially old people. Grandma was an old lady. And she was ill.

Joanna was full of her usual plans, though she was mysterious with Peter and wouldn't tell him anything until James and Ian, and then one or two of the Wildcats, arrived at the vicarage. Then they divided into their groups, with the Wildcats going up into Jo's room and the Rats staying in the downstairs TV den. Mrs Smythe had arrived to cook and clean, and was busy mopping black marks off the hall floor.

"I don't know how you do it, Jo and James and the rest of you," she complained as they trailed through. "If there's any mud and dirt to be found, you'll find it and walk it in all over my floors."

"Sorry," said Jo. "I meant to clean up last night but I forgot. I'll wash up after every meal today, to make up. And we'll all be back in school again next week, Mrs Smythe."

"And a good thing too!" grumbled Mrs Smythe, but Tom could tell that she wasn't really cross with Jo.

He only half-listened to what the others were saying. Part of him was anxiously waiting for the Vicar to come home. He must talk to him about Grandma, he really must. He was dreadfully worried about her all of a sudden.

He noticed at once when the Vicar's car drove up and stopped outside in the driveway. The other Wildcats had arrived and were all there, sprawled over Jo's bed and on the floor, reading comics and magazines and eating chocolate crunch made by Mrs Smythe, as well as making plans. No one noticed when Tom slipped out of the room and went downstairs.

The hall was spotless and empty. Sounds of a food mixer and pleasant cooking smells came from the kitchen, and TV noises from the den across the hall. Tom went to the study door and knocked on it.

The Reverend Southcott was wearing reading glasses and looked surprised to see him.

"Oh, hello. Tom, isn't it? Did you want me?"

"Yes," said Tom. "Please could I go to church?"

The Vicar's eyebrows lifted. "Of course. We'd be delighted to have you. Sunday morning service is 11 am, evening worship 6 pm. There's Children's Church during the morning service. I've got a programme somewhere about."

He rummaged among the papers on his desk.

"No," said Tom. "I can't wait until Sunday. I mean now."

The Vicar took off his glasses and rubbed his forehead in a puzzled way. "That's a bit difficult, I'm afraid, just at the moment. Would you like to tell me why you're in such a hurry? Come in and sit down for a moment."

The Vicar closed the door behind them. Tom sat in a big chair at one side of the desk and the Vicar sat in the other. The study was untidy and cluttered, though not nearly as bad as Joanna's room.

The Vicar leaned forward, his fair hair flopping over his forehead. Without the glasses, his eyes were the same colour as Jo's, but he didn't have freckles like her. He said, "Is there something that's worrying you, Tom?"

"Yes," said Tom. And then suddenly he was telling the Vicar all about moving to the new house and leaving Grandma behind, and about Grandma's illness and his fears for her, and how important he felt it was to pray for her in church.

The Reverend Southcott listened carefully. He said, when Tom had finished, "I see. I'm sorry about your grandma. You and I will pray for her, shall we? You don't need to be in church, you know. You can talk to God just wherever you happen to be."

"Yes, I know," said Tom. "Grandma always told me that. Only – only I thought God would like it better if we were in church— "

"Not at all," said the Vicar. "God loves us always, all the time, wherever we are, just the same. He's delighted when we pray to him about anything, big or little. So shall we ask him about helping Grandma to get well?"

Tom hesitated. "Yes. You do it, please."

"If you like. But you can too, you know."

"Yes, I know," said Tom. "Grandma told me."

"I'd quite like to meet your Grandma," said the Vicar. "But something's still worrying you, isn't it?"

"Yes," said Tom. And then he said, all in a rush, "You see, God might not listen to me. Because – because yesterday I told Mum a fib. A big fib."

"Ah," said the Vicar. "I see. And you think God will be cross about that and won't want to listen to you and answer your prayers."

"Yes," said Tom. He held his breath, gripping the edge of the chair with both hands.

"Well," said the Vicar. "You're wrong there. God loves us always, no matter what we've done. We'll never be punished for our wrong things if we ask God to forgive us. That's because Jesus, God's son, was punished instead of us when he died. Do you understand?"

Tom thought for a moment, wrinkling his forehead. Then he said "You mean, like once when Peter and me were playing and some green paint got tipped on the best chair, and Mum was going to smack us, but Peter said it was his fault, so she only smacked him?"

The Vicar smiled. "Yes, that's it. When we've told him we're sorry for what we've done we are friends with him again. Then we can tell him what's worrying us and we know that he will listen."

Tom gave a sigh of relief. "Are you sure?"

"Quite sure. Take my word for it. I've known God for a long time."

Tom swung his legs, feeling suddenly light and free. He smiled across the desk at Jo's dad. The Vicar stretched his hand across the desk and took Tom's, and they both prayed together about Grandma.

Chapter fourteen
In the Rat's den

Tom came out of the study just as Joanna came galloping down the stairs. She looked very surprised to see him there.

"Oh, hello. I wondered where you'd gone. Whatever were you doing in there? We're not allowed, you know."

Now that his worry about Grandma had been brought out into the open and shared, Tom felt suddenly very light-hearted. He said, "I'm allowed. I've been talking to your dad and he says I can go and speak to him again whenever I want."

"Are you sure?"

"Course. Ask him, if you don't believe me."

"Oh, I believe you. Listen, you seem to be good at sneaking about and getting into places you're not supposed to. How would you like to be a spy?"

Tom wasn't sure. "What would I have to do?"

"Just keep your eyes and ears open. We want to find out whether those Rats know about the key. Would Peter have told them, do you think?"

Tom didn't know.

"Well, perhaps you could find out," said Jo. "It could make a difference. Some of us will have to go shopping, because we've planned something special for tonight. But if they know we've tricked them, they'll be expecting something and they'll be ready for us. It gives us less time to plan."

Tom felt rather confused by all this. He repeated, "What do I have to do?"

"For a start, pop along to the den and have a listen outside the door. See if you can hear anything. Then come back and report to us. If anyone asks, you can always say you're looking for your brother or something. In the meantime, I'll send Sam and Katie out to Tesco's."

Tom was more confused than ever. He thought it easiest not to ask any more questions but just do as Joanna told him. While she ran upstairs again, he went along the hallway to the door of the den and listened. From the outside, you would never have known that a desperate Rat Pack was gathered inside. The sounds that came out were just like a group of boys playing computer games, squabbling now and then, shouting and scuffling around. Tom tried his best to hear if anything about keys was being mentioned, but there was nothing, only bursts of cheering if someone scored and jeering if they did badly.

Suddenly the door flew open and James himself came out, almost falling over Tom and looking very surprised to see him.

"Hello. What're you doing there? Have you got a problem?"

"No," said Tom, but he couldn't think of anything else to say. The other Rats were peering round to see who James was talking to.

"Tired of playing with your dolls?" asked Ian.

Tom felt his cheeks grow red. For a moment he wished he'd joined the Rats while he had the chance. It wasn't much fun being lumped together with girls all the time.

"No," he said. "I was just looking for my brother."

Peter's face appeared over the back of a sofa. "What's the matter? You feeling sick or something?"

Tom shook his head.

"Well then, stop following me around. Hop it!"

"Yes, hop it!" said James. "Don't forget, it's nearly dark and when darkness falls, you know what happens. We become the Rat Pack. And when that happens, I wouldn't hang around on your own, if I were you. Not if you know what's good for you."

Tom was beginning to hop it. But, just as the door was closing behind him, James seemed to think twice. He pulled the door open again and seized Tom by the arm, pulling him back into the room. Then he closed the door and leant against it, folding his arms and looking thoughtfully at Tom.

"On second thoughts," he said, "I think we'll keep you here for a bit."

"I was going back upstairs," said Tom.

"All in good time," said James, "after we've finished with you. I think you've played into our hands, coming snooping around like that. I think you might be useful to us."

Tom hoped that he was not going to be taken to the dungeon again. Mum might put her foot down if he came home covered with coal dust a second time.

But James was pointing towards a beanbag near the TV.

"Sit down there."

Tom sat. His heart was beginning to beat faster. What were they going to do to him?

Everyone was looking expectantly at James, the computer game forgotten. It was beginning to grow dark outside. James reached across and switched off the light, plunging the room into gloom lit only by the flickering TV screen. He came and sat down opposite Tom.

"Now," he said. "I've had this funny feeling all day that those Wildcats are up to something. Giving us funny looks and giggling all the time, the way girls do. They can never keep a secret, that's their trouble. I want information. You tell us what they're planning, and we let you go free."

Tom looked from one face to another. They looked back at him, a circle of boys' faces, blue-white in the flickering light of the screen. Only – suddenly, they weren't boys' faces any longer. Darkness had come, everything had changed, and the group of ordinary boys had become the Rat Pack.

Tom found himself clutching the corduroy fabric of the beanbag with both hands. Looking from one face to another he could see in the dim flickering light that they all had pointed twitching noses, yellowish teeth and fangs, small beady eyes and grey-brown rat-coloured hair. They showed their teeth in horrible rat-like grins. Even Peter looked like a rat.

"Tell us," said the King Rat. "Tell us what you know."

Tom found his voice. "I don't know anything."

It was true. Jo had hinted that something was afoot, and she had mentioned something about shopping at Tesco's, but he hadn't a clue what it was all about.

"That's not good enough," said the King Rat softly. "You have to tell us. Or— "

He did not finish the sentence, but Tom had the impression that all the other rats looked at each other and twitched their whiskers, licked their lips and sniggered.

Would Jo come and rescue him, if he shouted loud enough? But that hope soon died. "If you're thinking of squealing," said King Rat, "I might as well tell you you won't be heard. This room is soundproof."

Tom saw that it was hopeless. But he couldn't tell them anything because he didn't know. Should he make up a story, anything, just so they'd let him go and not do some terrible torture to him? He had a horrible sick feeling in his stomach that they were capable of anything.

He looked at the circle of grinning rat-faces again. Then, suddenly, he noticed something on the carpet near the King Rat's chair. A blue helmet, and pushed inside it, a pair of blue and yellow cycling gloves.

He remembered that day he'd been lost – was it only yesterday? – all alone and anxious about Grandma and not even able to remember his address and telephone number. That boy in the blue helmet had come along at just the right moment, had helped him and walked along with him until he was safely at Jo's house. That boy had been nice and kind, he would never hurt or torture anyone.

Suddenly he sat up straighter, not scared anymore. He said, "I'm not telling you anything because I don't know anything. And I think I'll go back upstairs again now."

He got up and walked over to the door. No one tried to stop him. At the doorway, he flicked on the light switch again. He paused for a moment, looking back at the others. Suddenly, the circle of people sitting there weren't rats after all, just a group of bigger boys blinking in the bright light and looking rather puzzled.

Chapter fifteen
The plan

"You've been a long time," said Joanna. "What happened?"

"Nothing much," said Tom. "They dragged me in and asked me what you were planning to do. I think they were going to torture me. But I wouldn't tell them, so they let me go."

"You're getting to be a dreadful fibber," said Jo. "But never mind, it's all good fun. Have you got anything to report to me, that's the main thing?"

Tom said he hadn't, except that the Rat Pack thought they were up to something.

"Never mind," said Jo. "Everything's ready. We've made our plans and they're fool-proof. We're a match for those Rats any day."

Two bulging plastic bags stood by the door, and Jo was busily collecting paper plates and cups and stuffing them into another bag.

"What are we going to do?"

"My favourite thing," said Jo. "A feast! A great big, scrumptious feast in the shed. In OUR shed. To celebrate taking it back again. I expect they'll try to butt in, but we'll be ready to repel them!"

Katie was sent to keep watch by the den door

while Jo hunted about in the kitchen cupboards and found a camping stove, fuel, matches, a saucepan and frying pan and some rock buns and cup cakes which Mrs Smythe had made before finishing work for the day and going home. They left the house quietly in single file, each carrying a load and taking the long route round the house to avoid both the den and the study windows.

The weather was still as chilly as ever, and there was a new moon just showing in the darkening sky. The shrubbery was dark and mysterious, full of small rustlings and whisperings. A prowling tomcat yowled from over by the hedge, and Tom jumped. It was a real cat this time.

"One of our brothers," said Jo. "Wishing us well."

They let themselves in with the spare key and crowded into the dim, musty, draughty shed. It seemed cold and lonely. Tom shivered. He wondered again why the place was so special that both the Rats and the Wildcats wanted it so badly. Beyond the shrubbery, the lights of Jo's room, which they'd forgotten to switch off, sent a beam into the darkness. It had been cosy there, with the music and clutter and the warmth of the heating. He'd have been quite happy to stay there until it was time to go home.

But Jo's plan must go ahead. She locked the door behind them and wedged the torch in a position where it would throw most light. Katie and Kelly unpacked the Tesco bags, setting out bread rolls and frozen burgers and sausages, bottles of pop and chocolate biscuits. Jo set the little camping stove on the table under the window and struggled to get it going. It was troublesome at first. Jo huffed and puffed, called the stove names, and in the end it responded by bursting into life, spluttering a few times and then settling down to burn with a steady blue flame.

"Now then," said Jo triumphantly. "Where's the pan? Burgers first, and then the sausages can go on to cook while we're eating them. No waiting between courses."

The burgers frizzled nicely in the pan and sent out a good meaty smell that made everyone feel hungry, though it was less than an hour since they'd had tea. It was difficult to tell in the dim light when they were cooked through, and Jo had to rely a great deal on guesswork. But they tasted good and only a little bit burnt when they were doled out, sandwiched between bread rolls. While they ate, sausages sizzled in the pan for the next part of the feast.

"Keep an ear open for those Rats," said Jo with her mouth full. "We're not giving them anything, not a single crumb, not even if they plead on bended knees."

Katie poured pop into plastic cups and handed it round. The sausages spluttered in the pan. Then Sam reached across the table for the pop bottle, and her arm nudged the edge of the pan.

"Watch out!" said Katie, and made a grab for it. She caught the pan and dropped it again as it burned her fingers. The pan hit the stove, tipped, and most of the sausages landed on the floor.

But some of the fat splashed onto the stove with a hissing sound. The steady blue flame turned into a leaping yellow one and shot suddenly upwards. Someone shrieked and they all gasped. The flame had jumped to meet the Rats' notice, the large piece of paper pinned to the wall, which was suddenly ablaze.

Chapter sixteen
Fire!

For a moment there was total confusion. Everyone stampeded to the far end of the shed away from the blaze, except Jo, who tried to put it out. She succeeded in smothering the stove with her anorak, which gave off a strong charred smell. But the burning paper on the wall flared up and set light to some old sacking and newspapers on a shelf above, which began to blaze at once, fanned by a draught from the open window space. Then flames were licking up the wooden walls of the shed itself.

Smoke tickled Tom's nose and throat and he began to cough.

"It's no good!" said Jo in a breathless gasp. "I can't put it out. Let's all get out of here."

Someone seized the shed door and rattled the handle, but it would not open. Then they remembered that they had locked it from the inside to keep out the Rats.

"The key!" said Jo. "Turn the key!"

But the key seemed to have fallen out and lost itself underfoot. Everyone scrabbled around looking for it on the floor, banging into each other and bumping heads. The key was nowhere to be seen.

"We can't get out!" wailed Katie suddenly. "We're trapped! We'll be burned alive!"

Panic was setting in. Someone screamed, Tom coughed again and so did someone else. Smoke was curling across the room. The flames were crackling around the window frame, licking and spreading up towards the roof of the shed. Bits of charred and burning paper and sacking floated about in the strong draught. Already they could feel the heat of the fire on their hands and faces.

Kelly, in tears, rattled vainly at the door handle.

"Jo, what are we going to do?"

"The key!" muttered Jo, still scrabbling about on the floor. "Wherever is that key?"

A lump of burning sacking fell from the shelf setting light to some seed boxes in the far corner, where a new fire sprang up. Now everyone seemed to be screaming. Tom was squashed into the corner by the door, behind several frightened Wildcats. His eyes stung and smarted and he coughed and coughed.

Then suddenly there was a new sound. Loud boys' voices above the screaming and coughing and spluttering in the shed. Something crashed hard into the door from outside. Then suddenly it was wrenched open on a blast of cold air and they were tumbling, falling, scrambling out into the frost and the dark and a ring of white, wide-eyed boys' faces.

Everyone stopped screaming and coughing and crying and became very quiet. Rats and Wildcats together watched in silence as the shed blazed and crackled and tumbled in upon itself, like the biggest Guy Fawkes bonfire they had ever seen. Tom and Peter had made a dive for each other and stood holding hands tightly. Tom had stopped coughing and, strangely enough, had stopped feeling frightened too. Some of the Wildcats were still sniffling quietly, and Ian offered a handkerchief to Katie, but no one called anyone else names. Tom saw that Jo and James were holding hands too, standing close together for comfort as he and Peter were. For once, neither of them seemed to have anything to say. The burning shed made a circle of light in the clearing and sent flickering shadows dancing against the dark leaves of the shrubbery bushes. The flames were blue and yellow and orange, licking up and devouring all that was left of the shed. The lean-to roof caved in and sent showers of sparks into the dark sky. One or two of the watchers gasped. Tom moved a little closer to Peter and Peter didn't move away.

Then the fire was crumbling and dying down, the flames subsiding. Where the shed had been was now a bed of hot red ash.

One of the Rats spoke. "Well, that's the end of that."

Kelly shuddered. "Thank goodness we got out in time."

The spell seemed broken. Suddenly everyone was talking at once. The Rats wanted to know how the fire had started, and how the Wildcats had got into the shed in the first place. The Wildcats, still light-headed with relief over their narrow escape, were inclined to jabber and not make much sense. Tom saw suddenly that Jo was in tears, sobbing and rubbing grimy knuckles into her eyes.

"It was all my fault! I tricked you about the key! I should've known better than to light a fire inside!"

To Tom's surprise, James put his arm around her and said "Don't cry. It was an accident. Please don't cry, Jo." Tom saw him stuff something into her hand. "Here, take this. It's your pouch thing. I picked it up outside the shed door. It isn't burnt at all, and I haven't looked inside, honest. I was going to, but— "

Jo took the pouch with one hand, pushing back her hair with the other. "I don't mind you seeing."

She opened the pouch and pulled out its contents. Everyone craned to look. Tom saw a crumpled letter or two, a lock of long fair hair tied with green ribbon, and a framed photograph. Standing at Jo's elbow, he had a quick glimpse in the firelight of the face of a young woman, sweet and smiling, with long hair swinging past her shoulders. Then James had taken the photo and was gazing at it.

"I don't suppose you remember her," said Jo gruffly.

"Of course I do," said James. "Auntie Jean. She was my very favourite Aunt. I loved her a lot."

And suddenly, he and Joanna were both snuffling in front of everyone and holding on to each other in a big hug.

Tom felt his own eyes stinging with tears and he saw that some of the Rats and Wildcats were blinking hard and shuffling their feet. For a while no one said anything.

Then one of the Wildcats said, "That's the end of our shed, anyway."

"OUR shed" said one of the Rats.

"Not much point in arguing over it any more," said Ian.

They all looked at the mound of smouldering,

flickering red ash.

"It wasn't much of a shed, anyway," said Katie with a sniff.

"Draughty old place," said Spike. "And cold."

"And dusty, and poky. Hardly room to turn round."

"Not worth fighting over, really."

"No."

"Still," said James. "The fighting was good fun while it lasted, wasn't it?"

Suddenly everyone was much more cheerful. Joanna dried her tears on her shirt sleeve and thanked James and the other Rats for saving the lives of the Wildcats. The Rats said casually that it was nothing, really, but they were kind enough not to poke fun at the Wildcats. They seemed impressed to learn about the extra key, which they hadn't known existed.

"And I was the only one who could climb through the window to get it," Tom told Peter importantly.

"I wondered why they wanted you," said Peter.

No one had thought that other people would have noticed the fire in the vicarage garden. They all jumped when the tall figure of the Vicar appeared on the path between the shrubs, carrying a strong torch and looking very worried.

"What on earth is going on?" he demanded in tones of horror, looking from the subdued group of children to the charred remains of his garden shed. "Joanna, what in the world have you gone and done NOW?"

Chapter seventeen
After the fire

There was a lot of explaining to be done. First of all, the Reverend Southcott checked that everyone was safe and accounted for and that the fire had died down enough not to need to call out the fire brigade. Then he shepherded them all into the vicarage kitchen and checked each child over to make sure that no one was burned, or singed, or hurt in any way. Then he made hot drinks all round. After that, he insisted on knowing every detail of what had happened to cause the burning down of his garden shed.

Jo took all the blame, and said that it was all her fault. "I'm sorry, Dad," she said miserably, suddenly seeming to Tom to be much smaller than usual. "I shouldn't have taken the stove and tried to cook in there. It was really stupid. We shouldn't have locked ourselves in. I should have had more sense. I'm sorry about your shed and the tools and things."

She wiped a tear from her grimy face with an even grimier finger. The Vicar patted her shoulder. "Never mind about the shed. I never liked it anyway. As for the tools, well, as you know, I'm always too busy to do any gardening. You're the important thing – you and the others. Thank God you're all safe. You're quite right, it was a stupid thing to do. But maybe we'll learn something from all this. Even awful experiences can have good come out of them. Let's try and put it behind us, and be a bit more sensible in future. Okay? That applies to you too, James. And the rest of you as well."

"Yes, Dad," said Jo with a gulp.

"Yes, Uncle David," said James.

The rest didn't quite know what to say, so said nothing. But Tom saw that Jo was beginning to look a bit better.

The Vicar sent them in relays to the downstairs cloakroom to wash the worst of the smoke and grime off themselves. He phoned their parents to tell them what had happened and then he despatched most of them on their homeward way.

He decided that he would have to take Peter and Tom home himself, to explain and apologise, as they were new to the district. A subdued Jo went with them.

Mum and Dad were just making a cup of tea, and Emma was building a dolls' house out of empty cardboard boxes. There was a strong smell of fresh emulsion paint in the air. Mum and Dad both seemed rather flustered to see the Vicar on the doorstep. He had already visited them, and they liked him very much, but he did look different in his jeans and without his Vicar's collar. They took him into the freshly-painted living room, and Mum got out the best cups and saucers, though Tom could have told her that the Vicar wouldn't have minded drinking tea from a mug like anyone else. Peter and Tom took Jo upstairs to their room, where they sat rather quietly in a row on Peter's bed with Rusty at their feet.

Jo broke the silence. "I don't suppose your mum will let you come to the vicarage any more, after this."

"She will," said Tom at once. "She likes you a lot. She says nearly every time she sees you what a nice girl you are. And responsible."

"I don't think she'll say THAT any more," said Jo sadly. She reached out to pat Rusty, who was leaning against her knee in a very comforting way.

Tom noticed that the thumb of her other hand was stroking the pouch at her belt with the picture of her mother in it.

"Well, I think you're nice, anyway," he said.

Secretly, Tom was rather afraid that Mum and Dad would be very cross too. But to his surprise, they chatted happily over tea with the Vicar for quite a long time, and everyone parted on the friendliest of terms, feeling that they had known each other for a long time.

"What a nice man the Vicar is," said Mum when they had left. "I think so every time I see him. You can see where Jo gets it from. He's doing a very good job of bringing her up all on his own. She's a real credit to him, and I told him so. Poor man, he was so apologetic about the boys being there when the garden shed burned down. It's very kind of him to let the children have the run of that lovely big garden. Keeps them from getting into mischief around the town, he says. Though he says he's going to have to be much stricter about matches and things like that."

She paused for breath, clearing away the tea

things. The boys looked at each other. They still feared that the vicarage would be forbidden territory from now on, and suddenly it seemed to matter very much.

But Mum continued, "I invited them both to come round to tea next Tuesday, when you children are all back at school. It would save him bothering about making a meal. And the Vicar enjoyed my shortbread so much that I thought I'd send some round when I make a fresh batch. You boys can take it next time you go. Jo's dad has made her promise never ever to play around with fire again. And that applies to you too, of course."

Dad cleared his throat. "We've been thinking," he said, his eyes on the two boys, "that maybe we ought to begin going to church as a family. We've always been impressed by the people at Grandma's church, and the way they help and care for one another. The people here at St John's seem to be the same. They've got an enquirers' group going, for people who want to understand more about God, and we thought we might go. Having just moved to a new home and a new job, now seems to be as good a time as any. We thought we might all go to St John's. What do you boys think? Would you like that?"

"Yes please," said Peter. "James goes. He's in the choir. Choir practice is a lot of fun, he says. And they have a thing called Childrens' Church, to go to when the boring talking bit comes on."

Mum and Dad smiled. "What about you, Tom?"

"Yes please," said Tom.

Chapter eighteen
Sunday

They all went to church together on Sunday morning, even Emma, though they left Rusty at home with a big bone to keep him company.

It was frosty again, but when they got to church the sun was coming out to melt the sprinkling of white on the grass in the shady places under the churchyard yew trees.

Tom was surprised to see how many of the Rats and Wildcats, and other children too, were in the service. Several of them were in the choir, with shining brushed hair and frilly things around their necks. There was James, looking less than ever like a King Rat, and Ian, Spike and Katie were in the congregation, with people who must be their families. He thought the choir boys looked a bit strange in their white dress-things, and it was a relief to see that the others looked the same as usual.

For a while Tom thought Joanna wasn't there at all. He craned his neck in every direction, but couldn't seem to find her anywhere in the church. Then he realised that a girl in the very front row was Jo. She looked so different, in a red jumper and skirt, with her honey-coloured hair rippling down her back in little waves from under a black velvet band, that he hadn't recognised her at first. Then she turned and smiled at him and Peter, and he knew who she was, though somehow she looked smaller than usual. Maybe it was because she wasn't wearing her peaked cap, and had smart black shoes on her feet instead of the usual Doc Martens. Anyway, she looked very pleased that they had come to St John's.

Tom was glad that they had come, too. He enjoyed the lively tunes they sang, though he didn't know all of them.

The service was a little different from the ones he'd been to with Grandma, but had the same good feeling. At one point, everyone got out of their seats and went round to talk to other people, asking how they were and hugging and kissing each other. Tom wasn't too keen on the hugging and kissing, but it gave him the feeling that he was noticed and cared about, that he mattered. A buzz of conversation broke out all over the church, and some of the Rats and Wildcats came up and spoke to him and Peter. Then everyone went back to their seats again. The Reverend Southcott looked like a real Vicar today, in his black and white robes, though his hair still flopped over his forehead and his smile was still the same.

Tom wouldn't have minded sitting right through the service and listening to what the Vicar said about Jesus. But a young man came and took them to Children's Church, in a room at the back. It was all right though, because he talked about Jesus too, and said some of the same things that Grandma had told Tom. Tom wondered how

Grandma was, and whether she was missing them badly. It was almost a week since they'd moved, though it felt much longer.

The children waited in the churchyard for a little while after the service, while the grown-ups talked. Tom saw that Mum and Dad were laughing and talking with a group of other parents. The choir boys had taken off their robes and were looking a lot more like their usual selves. They looked even more usual when two or three of them had a friendly scrap round the side of the church porch. Joanna stepped in to pull them apart, ignoring her Sunday best clothes.

"Cut it out!" she said bossily, and Tom was quite relieved to see that she seemed to be her usual self again too. "We need to talk," she went on. "I've been thinking. Now that the shed is gone, we need a new headquarters. All of us. I thought, maybe if we got together, we could design a new place and build it ourselves. What do you think?"

"You mean, join forces?" asked James doubtfully.

"Yes. It's a bit silly really, and babyish, all this Rats and Wildcats stuff, don't you think? All right for little kids, but some of us are in High School now. If we put our heads together, we could design a really good place. I drew a few plans last night. Have a look and see what you think."

She pulled a crumpled piece of paper from her pocket and spread it out on the top of a tombstone. She and James bent over it, heads together.

The rest of the Wildcats and Rats looked at each other. "You know what'll happen, don't you?" said Ian. "It'll be those two giving the orders and the rest of us doing the dirty work."

The others were inclined to agree. Yet somehow, none of them really disliked the idea of being one large gang instead of two smaller ones, always fighting each other. It might be a lot more fun, and less hard work in the long run. Tom thought it would be very nice to be on the same side as both Jo and Peter.

There was something he wanted to ask Peter, and he got the chance when they were walking up their own street after church, ahead of Mum and Dad and Emma.

"Did you tell the Rats about the other key?" he asked.

"No," said Peter. "I thought you might get into trouble. You're such a nitwit and so little."

Tom had to thump Peter to prove that he was not as little as all that, but it was only the kind of thumping that goes on between friends and not the serious sort.

Sunshine was flooding into the new house as they let themselves in. Mum had put a casserole in to cook, and good smells were coming from the kitchen. Tom noticed for the first time how very fresh and new everything looked now that Mum and Dad had almost finished decorating. The horrid beige paint had gone from the banisters and they were sparkling white against soft peach walls. The living room was now a pale yellow, reflecting the sunshine, and Mum had a pot of bronze chrysanthemums on the little round table in the window. Rusty got up from his basket and came to meet them, and suddenly it felt like home.

Grandma phoned as they were finishing lunch.

"Is it really Gran herself?" asked Tom.

"Yes," said Mum. "Each of you come and speak

for a few minutes."

Grandma sounded much the same as usual, and very cheerful. She said that she'd had 'flu and a touch of bronchitis, but was much better now. She asked what Tom had been doing all week.

"Nothing much," said Tom. "We've been playing at the vicarage. The other day the shed burned down. And today we all went to church."

"Goodness!" said Grandma. "You HAVE been busy! That all sounds exciting. Not still missing Brian and Kevin too much, then?"

Tom wrinkled his nose. He hadn't forgotten Brian and Kevin, exactly, but somehow they seemed a bit distant now. Part of the old life. "I miss them a bit," he said. "And I still miss you, Gran. I'm glad you're better. When you were ill the Vicar and I prayed for you. And he said he'd like to meet you."

"Thank you very much," said Grandma. "For your prayers, I mean. They were answered all right. I'd like to meet him, too. I expect I will, because I'm coming for a visit in a week or two."

"Yes!" said Tom. There was a whole lot more he wanted to tell Gran, but Mum took the phone from him and held it for Emma to speak next. Tom remembered that he'd started writing a letter to Grandma the day they'd arrived. He thought he'd finish it now and put in all the rest of his news.

He found the exercise book among the newspapers in the magazine rack and spread it out, frowning. He decided he'd have to start again, because the letter didn't really make sense now. They hadn't just arrived, they'd been here ages. The house wasn't cold and empty any more, but warm and full of life.

He tore up the paper and started again with another page.

"Dear Gran, We've been here nearly a week now. The house is all nice and brite. The boys here are quite nice when you get to know them. The Vicar has a nice big girl called Jo. I like living here very much ..."